Adapted by Michael Teitelbaum
Illustrated by Sue DiCicco

A GOLDEN BOOK • NEW YORK
Western Publishing Company, Inc., Racine, Wisconsin 53404

Library of Congress Catalog Card Number: 90-85637 ISBN: 0-307-12335-9 R MCMXCII

Triton, the great Sea King, had seven lovely daughters. The youngest, whose name was Ariel, worried her father deeply. Though King Triton had warned her never to visit the world above the water's surface, Ariel often disobeyed him.

Ariel and her friend Flounder liked to visit Scuttle the sea gull. Scuttle would tell them all about the human objects that Ariel discovered in wrecked ships at the bottom of the sea.

One day, when Triton found out that Ariel had been visiting above the water again, the Sea King grew angry. He was so worried about his daughter's safety that he asked his trusted friend Sebastian the crab to watch over Ariel.

A few days later Ariel noticed a ship sailing overhead, on the surface of the sea. "Human beings!" said Ariel, swimming quickly toward the ship. Sebastian and Flounder swam after her.

When Ariel reached the ship, she saw a handsome young sailor whom the other sailors called Prince Eric. It was love at first sight!

Suddenly the sky darkened. Heavy rain began to fall and lightning split the sky. Prince Eric's ship was no match for the terrible storm, and the prince was thrown overboard.

"I've got to save him!" thought Ariel. She struggled to pull the drowning prince up onto the beach. Prince Eric did not stir as Ariel gently touched his face and sang him a beautiful love song. Ariel then kissed the prince and dove back into the sea.

When Prince Eric awoke, he was surrounded by his crewmates. "A wonderful girl saved me," said the still-dazed prince. "She sang to me in the most beautiful voice I have ever heard. I want to find that girl and marry her!" Prince Eric, too, had fallen in love.

King Triton was furious when he discovered that his youngest daughter had fallen in love with a human being. He rushed to the cave where his disobedient child kept her collection of human treasures.

The little mermaid tried to reason with her father. "Daddy, I love him so!" she cried. "I want to be with him."

"NEVER!" Triton shouted. "He's a human being. A fish-eater!" The Sea King angrily destroyed all of Ariel's human treasures. Then the mighty Sea King left.

Ariel buried her face in her hands and wept.

Meanwhile, nearby, evil forces were at work. Ursula, a wicked Sea Witch who had ruled the kingdom before Triton, was looking for a way to regain power. She could see Ariel crying in her crystal ball, and an idea came to her. "I shall destroy the Sea King through his daughter," she said excitedly.

Ursula sent her slimy eel servants, Flotsam and Jetsam, to Ariel's cave. They convinced the little mermaid that Ursula could help her to win her beloved prince's love. Ariel swam off with Flotsam and Jetsam to meet the Sea Witch.

"I have a deal for you, my sweet child," began Ursula when Ariel entered the witch's lair.

"A deal?" asked Ariel innocently.

"Yes," said the witch. "I will make you human for three whole days. If you can get the prince to kiss you before the sun sets on the third day, you will be able to stay with him forever, as a human being. But, if he does not kiss you, then you will turn back into a mermaid . . . and you will belong to me!

"The price for this favor," the witch continued, "is your voice!"
"My voice?" asked Ariel in shock. "But then I won't be able to talk or sing. How will I get the prince to fall in love with me?"
"You still have your pretty face," replied Ursula. "It should be easy."

Ariel agreed to Ursula's deal and the Sea Witch cast her magic spell. An amazing change took place. Ariel lost her tail, grew legs, and became entirely human. At the same time, her voice flew from her body and was captured inside a seashell.

When she went to find the prince, Ariel was helped ashore by Sebastian, Scuttle, and Flounder, who still watched over their friend. She tried to speak to them, but no sound came.

Soon Ariel saw Prince Eric. He had been lovesick over her ever since he had heard her sing. At first the prince was sure Ariel was the girl who had rescued him, but when he learned that she couldn't speak, he thought he must be wrong.

Prince Eric felt sorry for Ariel, who seemed lost and all alone. He took her back to his palace.

During the next two days Prince Eric grew fond of Ariel. On a boat ride together, Eric was about to kiss Ariel when Flotsam and Jetsam overturned the boat.

On the morning of the third day, there was great excitement throughout the kingdom. Prince Eric was going to marry a young maiden he had just met! Unfortunately for Ariel, Eric was now under a spell. Using her magic, Ursula had disguised herself as a lovely young girl. And because she spoke with Ariel's voice—which she carried in a seashell worn around her neck—Eric believed that she was the girl who had saved him from drowning. Poor Ariel was heartbroken.

The wedding was to take place on a special wedding ship. Scuttle the sea gull flew over it just as the bride was passing in front of a mirror. Scuttle saw that her reflection was that of the Sea Witch! He rushed off to tell Ariel and her two loyal friends.

Sebastian quickly formed a plan. Flounder would help Ariel get to Eric's ship, and Scuttle would arrange for some of his friends to delay the wedding.

"I'm going to tell Triton about all this," said Sebastian.

Prince Eric and the maiden were standing at the altar about to be married when a flock of sea gulls swooped down. Scuttle pulled the seashell containing Ariel's voice from around the Sea Witch's neck. The shell shattered, and Ariel's voice returned to Ariel, who had just climbed on board.

"Oh, Eric, I love you," said Ariel.

"Then it was you all along!" said the delighted prince. But just as they were about to kiss, the sun disappeared over the horizon. Ariel's three days were up and she was changed back into a mermaid. The Sea Witch had triumphed after all. Ursula grabbed Ariel and dove off the ship.

Thanks to Sebastian's warning, Triton was waiting at Ursula's lair. "I'll let your daughter go," cried Ursula, "but only in exchange for you!" Triton agreed, and he became Ursula's prisoner. She now had his magic trident and controlled the undersea kingdom.

Suddenly a harpoon struck Ursula's shoulder. Prince Eric had come to rescue Ariel. The little mermaid swam to the surface with him. But Ursula followed close behind, growing bigger and angrier, until she rose out of the water.

Prince Eric swam to his ship and climbed on board. He grabbed the wheel and turned the prow toward Ursula. The Sea Witch was about to fire a deadly bolt at Ariel when the prince's vessel slammed into Ursula, destroying the evil witch.

Now that Ursula was dead, Triton was free. He rose from the sea, his trident back in hand. He could see Ariel watching over Prince Eric, who was lying on the shore, unconscious.

"She really does love him, doesn't she?" the Sea King asked.

Sebastian, who was nearby, nodded.

"I shall miss her," Triton said. Then he raised his trident and shot a magic bolt at Ariel's tail.

At once, the little mermaid's tail disappeared, and she was human once again. Prince Eric awoke to see his beloved Ariel standing beside him on the shore. He kissed her and soon they were married. Prince Eric and Ariel sailed off together, and they lived happily ever after.